Jamaica Is Thankful

*I am thankful for everyone who has made this book possible,
especially Mary Wilcox, Anne Sibley O'Brien, and Nancy Gallt.
—J.H.*

*For Lucia & Simone, Bella & Willow; thanks for your help.
—A.S.O'B.*

Text copyright © 2009 by Juanita Havill
Illustrations copyright © 2009 by Anne Sibley O'Brien

Houghton Mifflin Books for Children is an imprint of
Houghton Mifflin Harcourt Publishing Company.

www.hmhbooks.com

The text of this book is set in Sabon.
The illustrations are watercolor and pastel.

Library of Congress Cataloging-in-Publication Data is on file.

ISBN: 978-0-618-98231-8

Printed in Singapore
TWP 10 9 8 7 6 5 4 3 2 1

Jamaica Is Thankful

Juanita Havill
Illustrated by Anne Sibley O'Brien

Houghton Mifflin Books for Children
HOUGHTON MIFFLIN HARCOURT
Boston   New York   2009

"Hi, Kristin!" Jamaica opened the front door for her friend. Kristin was holding a big red shoebox. "Jamaica, I've got something to show you." Then she said in a quiet voice, "Maybe we should go to your room."

Kristin set the box on the floor in the middle of Jamaica's room. "Could you close the door?" she asked.

Jamaica pushed her door shut, then plopped down beside Kristin.

Kristin took the lid off the box. "Her name's Puffy. And I can't keep her."

"Oooh, Kristin. She is so cute." Jamaica reached into the box and touched the soft black and white kitten.

"Go ahead and pick her up."

Jamaica scooped up Puffy and held her close. She noticed that the bottom of the box was filled with sandy stuff. "Why can't you keep her?"

"Because our old cat MaBelle doesn't get along with Puffy. Mom says we had MaBelle first. We have to give Puffy back to Aunt Florence."

"Too bad," Jamaica said.

"Unless," Kristin said, "maybe you could keep her."

Jamaica frowned. "My brother, Ossie, is allergic to cats and dogs. That's why we don't have any."

"But Puffy's just a kitten. Ossie might not be allergic to her. Couldn't you ask?"

Jamaica thought for a moment. She stroked Puffy's soft fur. She scratched under Puffy's ears. "She's purring."

"She likes you," Kristin said.

"I like her, too," Jamaica said. "I guess it wouldn't hurt to ask. Mother isn't here right now, and Dad's working on the computer. I'll wait until he isn't busy."

"You can keep Puffy while you wait."

"I can?" Jamaica said. "Thank you. Thank you."

Jamaica put the shoebox in her closet. "This is Puffy's litter box, isn't it?"

Kristin nodded and took a small can of cat food from her backpack. "Until you have time to get some. She only eats a little."

They put water in a bowl for Puffy and watched her drink.

"Oh, cute," Jamaica said.

"Your dad just has to say yes," Kristin said. "Then I can come and see Puffy at your house."

After Kristin left, Jamaica went to ask Dad, but he was on the phone. When she went back to her room, Puffy was scratching at the door.

"Shhh," Jamaica opened the door a crack and slipped into her room. "Are you hungry, Puffy?" she whispered. She dished out some food on one of her play dishes and set the dish on the closet floor. Puffy ate all the food.

"You were hungry, weren't you, Puffy?" Jamaica watched the kitten wash her face with her paw, then curl into a little ball on a shirt on the floor.

"Hey, Jamaica!"

Jamaica scrambled from the closet when she heard Ossie's voice. She shut the closet door behind her.

Ossie stepped into her room. "What's with the closed door?"

"Oh, I was just playing," Jamaica said.

Ossie shrugged. "I've got a game today, and I can't find my football jersey. Do you have my old one? I gave it to you last year."

"It's in the closet. I'll get it."

Jamaica opened the closet door a crack. "But you can't come in, Ossie."

"Why not?"

"Because it's secret. I'll tell you later." She squeezed in, then closed the door.

Puffy was still curled up, asleep, on Ossie's football jersey. Jamaica slid the shirt gently from underneath the sleeping kitten. Puffy didn't even wake up.

She slipped out the closet door. "Here, Ossie."

"Thanks." Ossie pulled on the jersey. "Do you want to catch some passes? I need to warm up my arm."

"Let's go," Jamaica said.

Ossie and Jamaica lobbed the ball back and forth a few times. Then Ossie told Jamaica, "Run for a pass."

"Okay!" Jamaica started running, then turned and saw the ball coming really fast. "Oof." It bumped against her chest, but she held on to it.

"Good catch, Jamaica."

Jamaica threw the ball back to Ossie, but she didn't throw it far enough. Ossie ran toward it. He reached for the ball, sneezed—"*Ah-choo!*"—and missed. "*Ah-choo! Ah-choo!*"

"I'll get it, Ossie."

Jamaica ran up and grabbed the ball. She turned to throw it to Ossie, but he was rubbing his eyes.

"Are you getting a cold, Ossie?"

"No, it's my allergy. I don't know why. I haven't been around any dogs or—*ah-choo!*—cats."

Ossie had been near Puffy, Jamaica thought. But he did say "cats," not "kittens." Puffy was only a kitten.

Dad called from the back door, "Maurice is here.
His mother is driving you to the game."

"Gotta go," Ossie said to Jamaica.

Dad waved Ossie's jersey. "It was in my office."

Ossie changed jerseys and tossed his old one to
Jamaica. "See you at the game," he said.

When Jamaica went back to her room and opened the closet door, Puffy bounced around her. Jamaica picked her up and set her on the bed. She lay down, and Puffy played with her braids. It tickled.

"How can anyone be allergic to you, Puffy?" she said.

But Ossie's eyes had been red and watery, and he had sneezed and sneezed. He hadn't even touched Puffy. All he had done was wear the football jersey Puffy had slept on. Even if Puffy was only a kitten, Ossie would sneeze. Even if he liked Puffy, his eyes would be red and swollen.

"Dad, do I have time to go to Kristin's?" Jamaica asked. She was holding the red shoebox with Puffy in it. "I have to take something back to her."

Jamaica took the lid off the box.

"She left her kitten?" Dad said.

"Just for a little while. Her name is Puffy. Isn't she cute?"

"All kittens are cute," Dad said. He stroked Puffy's head. "Good thing Ossie isn't here."

"I know," Jamaica said.

"Why don't you ask Kristin to come to the game?"

Kristin came to the door when Jamaica rang the doorbell. She looked at the shoebox. "You can't keep Puffy, can you?"

Jamaica handed the box to Kristin. "I wish I could."

"Now I'll have to take Puffy back to Aunt Florence." Kristin sighed. "Mom says I should be thankful for MaBelle."

"You should be thankful to have a cat. I can't ever have a cat because Ossie's allergic."

"At least you have a brother," said Kristin.

Kristin doesn't have a brother, Jamaica thought. Then she said, "I like my brother—even more than Puffy."

Jamaica and Kristin cheered for Ossie at the game. He threw a long pass to a teammate, who scored.

"Way to go, Ossie," Jamaica said.

After the game Kristin told Ossie, "You know what, Ossie? Jamaica says she likes you better than Puffy."

"I do," said Jamaica.

"Cool," said Ossie. "Who's Puffy?"

"How about I tell you tomorrow," Jamaica said, "when we play football together."